Emily

Brides of Montana
Book One

Cheryl Wright

Emily

Brides of Montana – Book One

Copyright ©2020

by Cheryl Wright

Small Town Romance Publications

Dedication

To Margaret Tanner, my very dear friend and fellow author, for her enduring encouragement and friendship.

To Alan, my husband of over forty-nine years, who has been a relentless supporter of my writing and dreams for many years.

To You, my wonderful readers, who encourage me to continue writing these stories. It is such a joy knowing so many of you enjoy reading my stories as much as I love writing them for you.

Table of Contents

Chapter One

Spring

Grand Falls, Montana - 1880

Emily Stanton swept the dirt and debris away from the front door of the boarding house.

W.J. Stanton and Sons had been in her family for over fifty years. The worn and sign still stood over the door. Not as proudly as it once had, but it was there, nonetheless.

She had recently repainted the second half of the sign to make it more visible.

Clean Rooms for Discerning Gentlemen

She didn't want any riffraff to apply, and neither had her father, or indeed, her grandfather. They only allowed upstanding young gents who would behave themselves and pay their rent on time.

In return, Emily would clean their rooms, make their beds, and supply a cooked breakfast and evening meal. Packed lunches would be provided for a little extra.

Speaking of cooked meals, she needed to go to the Mercantile and the Butcher Shop and buy the necessary items for tonight's meal.

She would have six hungry men chomping at the bit come supper time, and their food needed to be ready on time.

Six-thirty every night without fail their meal was placed in front of them. Once the prayers of thanks had been said, they tucked in.

She looked up at the freshly painted sign. Father would be pleased she had continued on with the business. Mother perhaps not so much. She'd hated this place. Hated having to do most of the hard work because of course, it was women's work.

According to Father anyway.

He usually pottered around making minor repairs, napping in-between jobs while Mother did all the hard and endless work. Emily did her share even before she left school. At least it had taken the pressure off Mother.

And now? Now she was doing it all alone. Some days were harder than others, but what choice did she have?

She glanced across at the broken chair sitting in the corner. What she needed was a man who could do all the necessary repairs, but finding someone like that in Grand Falls had proven to be impossible.

The only carpenter in town was far too busy building cottages to attend to small, tedious jobs like hers.

After putting the broom back where it belonged, she pulled on her bonnet, and readied herself to for shopping.

This was her daily routine after cooking and serving breakfast, doing the clean up afterwards, and making all the beds. If she was extra quick, Emily got to sit down and have a cup of tea or coffee before leaving the house. Most often coffee – it's what the men preferred, and there was usually left-overs.

After her parents had died, the people of Grand Falls had snickered at her decision to keep the boarding house going.

They thoroughly objected to a young, single woman running a boarding house full of men. She'd had a strong lock fitted to her private apartment for her own peace of mind.

She vowed to keep the family business going. After all, it wasn't her fault she was born female.

Of course she could have sold the business, but Father would have rolled over in his grave. On the other hand, she could imagine the smile on Mother's face. And there was no doubt in Emily's mind her mother would be nodding profusely.

Mother would have been more than happy to wipe her hands of the place back in her day.

Emily sighed. She was an upstanding young woman of high moral values. She would be safe she'd told the naysayers, and she'd proven that to be so. She'd not once had a problem with one of her boarders.

The rules were clear – no women on the premises, no alcohol, and no fraternizing with management.

Meaning Emily.

In addition, rent must be paid on time or they would be asked to leave immediately. So far there had been no problems with any of the rules.

Most of her young gentlemen were happy to have a roof over their heads, and food in their bellies. They were also quite protective of her. Not that she'd ever really needed help in that area. Not really.

Although there was that one time… No, she preferred not to think about it.

The majority only stayed long enough to secure long-term employment in the area, and had moved on soon after.

There were times when the house wasn't full, but provided she was able to cover her costs and have a little left over, Emily was happy. She was building a nice little nest egg for her future by depositing her profits into the local bank.

So far she hadn't needed to dip into her savings, but she knew it was inevitable. If she could find someone to do the repairs needed around the place, at least she would have the money to pay him. And right now, there were lots of repairs to be done.

Cecil Delbert from the Mercantile had been a dear and allowed her to put a notice in the window of his store for a carpenter or someone who could do repairs. So far there had been no takers.

No one in Grand Falls was qualified or had the necessary skills. With the town's influx of newcomers, she hoped that would change soon, but she wasn't holding her breath.

* * *

Patrick Harper stared out the window of the clattering train.

In the light of day, the scenery was nice. You could even call it pretty. In the cold hard cover of night, it looked quite frightening through the dusty windows.

He'd tried to sleep, but the jolting of the train in addition to the excitement of his new venture had caused sleep to be fleeting.

Patrick had been contracted to build new homes and businesses in the suddenly expanding Grand Falls. It would be quite busy to begin with, he was certain. At least until they caught up with demand.

This was a whole new venture, and one he had prayed for over many years.

Hard work and diligence had finally brought this to fruition.

There had been no time to arrange accommodation. Nor did he know if or where he would find any. He might end up staying at the hotel – assuming Grand Falls had a hotel, that was.

He shifted in his seat. He'd been on this rickety contraption for a little under twenty-four hours, but was wholly sick of it. He felt sorry for those who were doomed to longer trips.

The conductor strolled past on his way to the next carriage. "Excuse me," Patrick said, looking up at the uniformed gent. "How much further is it until we reach Grand Falls?"

"Not long, Sir. Another twenty minutes and we'll arrive." He touched his hat and was on his way before Patrick could thank him.

Twenty minutes. That wasn't too bad; he could endure that. He stretched his legs as far as he could, but it wasn't enough. So instead, he stood and stretched.

Stretching his arms upwards, his fingertips touched the roof of the train. He quickly pulled them away. It was good to stand, even if only for a few minutes.

He didn't dare move from his seat for fear his bag of tools would be stolen. His main luggage had been placed with the rest of the passenger's luggage, but he couldn't risk losing the tools of his trade.

Not only were they expensive to replace, but it would take forever for them to arrive. No, he would stay right where he was.

He craned his neck and glanced along the walkway between the seat. A number of other passengers were doing the same – stretching their legs before reaching the next station. After this amount of time limbs went numb, making it difficult to disembark.

He stared out the window again then returned to his seat. Grand Falls was said to be bigger than Dayton Falls, where he'd just left after working with his brother who was a baker there. Building and setting up his shop and home had taken quite some time, but it had been satisfying work.

Grand Falls promised to be satisfying too. Perhaps even more so.

Patrick was really looking forward to this new chapter in his life. But first he needed to find accommodation at an affordable price.

* * *

Strolling along the sidewalk after arriving at his destination, Patrick surveyed the town. It was far bigger than Dayton Falls, but not as large as he'd envisioned.

He felt a little dismayed, but then remembered there were contracts for several houses and stores.

He grinned.

Hard work and diligence. That's what Father had preached his entire life. After he had gone, his brother Ethan had told him the same. He ought to know – he had his own bakery store in Dayton Falls now. And what's more, Patrick had been paid to build it and the adjoining house.

He glanced around and spotted the diner, the bank, and the office to the saw mill. He stopped when he stood outside the Mercantile. The large poster in the window caught his eye:

Carpenter Needed

Well he was a carpenter, but he already had work lined up, so he was far from interested. Despite that, his eyes continued to scan the information.

It was signed *Emily Stanton, Owner*, and was on the letterhead for a boarding house. That part really piqued his interest.

He checked the address carefully. Stanton Way, Grand Falls.

Hmmm. The street was obviously named after an ancestor. Now all he had to do was find it.

He was about to enter the Mercantile and ask for directions when he almost collided with a young woman who was leaving.

"Excuse me," he said, staring at her amazing brown eyes. "Can you direct me to Stanton Way?"

She pursed her lips. "As it happens, I am heading that way myself." She had her hands full, and so did Patrick, so he was unable to offer to assist with her packages.

He indicated his overladen hands. "I apologize, Ma'am. I would help you if I could."

She looked down at his luggage. "You're new in town."

It wasn't a question, it was a statement. In a town this size, no doubt everyone knew everyone else. "Yes Ma'am. Just arrived," he said.

"Do you have business here?"

She was nosy, that was for sure, but Patrick didn't mind. Not really. It was a good way to get to know a local. "Yes Ma'am. I'm joining Harry Johnson with building new houses."

She turned to him and grinned. "Sawdust Harry, do you mean?" He could have sworn she was holding back peals of laughter.

"That's cute," he said, trying not to laugh himself. "I wonder what they'll call me?" It was his turn to grin.

"Ooooh, you're a carpenter too?" She looked more than a little relieved. Curious.

She stopped where she stood and waited for his response. He frowned, then put down his luggage. "Patrick Harper," he said, extending his hand and grinning. "Carpenter extraordinaire."

She juggled her shopping around and shook his hand. "Emily Stanton. I don't suppose you're looking for accommodation?"

"Yes Ma'am, I certainly am. I'm particularly keen on a boarding house that supplies meals."

He was a hopeless cook, and besides, when would he have the time to make meals? It made perfect sense.

"You have no idea how happy I am to meet you Mr Harper."

He stared at her. Her eyes were so mesmerizing, but it was more than that. Although Patrick couldn't put his finger on it. "The notice about the carpenter was from you?" Everything suddenly fell into place. "Perhaps I can help out, but I won't have a lot of time. I start work on Monday."

She sighed. "That doesn't give you much time." She picked up her packages again and Patrick did the same. As they turned into an alleyway, Emily indicated a building ahead of them. "That's us," she said, and picked up pace.

"Does that mean you have a room I can rent?" His heart quickened. He had no idea it would be this easy.

She glanced across at him. "I have only the one room available. You have great timing." She relieved herself of her shopping again and rummaged in her reticule for her keys. Once located, she unlocked the door and ushered Patrick inside.

He left his luggage in the entrance and hurried back to assist Emily with her shopping. Patrick wasn't sure why, but he felt drawn to her.

Then again, it could just be that he was being a proper gentleman. He'd probably never know which one it was.

"Through there, if you don't mind," she told him, indicating he take her shopping through to the kitchen. It was tiny compared to the massive kitchen he'd built for his brother back in Dayton Falls. But on the other hand, that kitchen was gigantic compared to most.

He glanced around. The kitchen really was quite small, and it would be difficult for more than one person to work in here. It could be far better with a few adjustments and some repairs.

He kept his opinion to himself.

"Come with me and I'll take you to your room," Emily said, snatching up a set of keys. "You'll be in room five – it's been empty for a few weeks, so I had a chance to thoroughly clean it." She glanced across at him and grinned. "It also happens to be the biggest of the rooms we have here." She fiddled with the keys for a moment, then opened the door. She pushed ahead of Patrick and tried to open the window to air the room out, but it was stuck. Probably from lack of use.

"Here, let me," he said, and his hand brushed against hers as he tried. Her skin was soft, and he loved the feel of it. She leaned closer trying to see what was wrong with it and he breathed in her fragrance.

He stepped back. He was not here to breathe in the essence of Miss Stanton.

"It's was working fine before Mr Credent left."

"It's probably just the change of weather." He suddenly let go. "I'll grab my tools. I'll be back momentarily."

He felt her eyes on his back and tried to ignore it. He brought his luggage and tools into his new place of abode. "You haven't by chance painted the window recently?" He looked at her curiously.

Her hands flew to her mouth. "I have," she said, sounding rather guilty. "I'm sorry."

"No need to be sorry." He reached into his toolbox and soon had the window moving freely again. "Some paint got into the tracks. All fixed."

She looked beyond relieved. "Thank you. I'll introduce you to the other lodgers at supper. They're all at work now."

She handed him the set of keys, which consisted of a room key and front door key.

She pointed out where everything was, not that there was much, then excused herself to begin work on supper.

"Wait," he shouted to her back. "I haven't paid you yet." As a matter of fact, he had no idea how much it was even going to cost him.

She looked back over her shoulder. "You've already earned your first day here by fixing the window. I have plenty more where that came from, so if you're agreeable…"

He frowned at her. That wasn't fair – he wanted to pay his way and not take advantage of this hardworking woman.

She stopped in her tracks. "Is that a no? You don't want to help?"

The distress on her face made him feel more than a little guilty. "I don't mind helping, but I must pay my own way. Tell me what the weekly rent is so I can pay it." He realized he sounded quite forceful. It wasn't his intention, but he needed to let her know how he felt.

"I, I'm sorry," she said, her voice breaking. "I didn't mean to assume. I'm rather desperate for help." She was talking quickly and he had to concentrate on her words. "I have a broken chair, damaged bookshelves. The kitchen cupboards need fixing…"

He felt bad now that he'd refused her. "I noticed the kitchen cupboards." He stepped toward her. "Perhaps we can come to some sort of agreement, but I won't allow you to give me free board."

He held her gently by the shoulders. "Is that understood?"

She nodded her agreement, and he stared down into her face. He saw her properly for the first time – she was an incredibly beautiful woman, but she was also harried. He had held her up, and now she was becoming anxious.

"I must go and prepare supper," she said, pulling out of his grip and stepping away. "We can talk more later."

Touching her had been magical. Patrick had never felt like this before. When their hands connected on the window, a thrill had gone down his spine.

When he looked into her face just now, his heart pounded. One thing was for certain, he needed to keep his distance. He was here to work, and for no other reason.

He wasn't sure how he could keep away when he'd promised to fix all the problems around the building. Perhaps he needed to look for somewhere else to stay.

The truth was, he didn't want to leave. He really liked Miss Emily Stanton, and they'd only just met.

Chapter Two

Standing at the head of the table, Emily introduced Patrick to the other lodgers. "Everyone, this is Patrick Harper. He has occupied room five."

All heads turned their way. "This is George, Aaron, Jesse, Zachary…" The names all became a blur. It wasn't Patrick's strong point, that was for sure, but he would soon learn them.

"You sit there," she said, indicating an empty chair at the other end of the table. "Supper won't be long."

The other men reached for the bread, so Patrick did the same. Butter sat in the center of the table, and was passed around.

Soon supper sat in front of each man, then they bowed their heads, and Emily said a prayer of thanks.

Supper was a noisy affair. He'd never sat at a table with so many people. He'd grown up with just the four in their family, so this was an eye-opener.

He knew for sure there were families bigger than his. The Piker family down the road had ten children. He was sure glad he wasn't part of that family.

Patrick glanced down at his plate. The food was good. Emily was a good cook – she'd no doubt had plenty of practice. "This is good," he heard himself say.

He looked up to see her blushing.

The other lodgers stared at him. Did no one here ever compliment her cooking? If that were so, it was a sad state of affairs. The fact they were paying rent did not negate politeness.

"Thank you," she said quietly, then dipped her head.

When the main course was over, she began to collect up all the soiled dishes. Patrick jumped up and began to help. "You don't need to do that," she said.

He paused momentarily and felt the collective glares before he saw them. "I don't mind. In fact I prefer to help," he said, ignoring the stares from around the table.

He followed her into the kitchen.

"Just put them in there," she said, indicating the sink. She turned and snatched up several of the desserts that were waiting on the counter top. He followed suit.

"You honestly don't have to do that," she said, a slight blush coming to her cheeks. "I've been doing it alone for many years."

He stared at her momentarily. "A burden shared…" He let the words hang between them, and she nodded.

They returned to the dining room and all talk suddenly stopped. He helped hand out the desserts, then took his place. All eyes were on him.

Why didn't these men like him helping out? Did they think they were above all that? He was brought up differently. His mother had worked hard in his father's bakery and everyone pitched in at home.

Like it or not, he would continue to help whenever he was able.

Starting with that kitchen. Not only did it look terrible, it was a hazard. Emily's gown could easily get caught up in the parts of the door that were currently swinging around.

He groaned inwardly. How had she even managed to work in such a hazardous place? He knew that answer was she had no choice.

He helped clear the dessert dishes away, and surveyed the kitchen again. "I'll take a look at those cupboard doors tomorrow."

She glanced up at him. "You don't have to do that."

"I know, but I want to. I hate the thought of you working in here with them like that. It's not safe."

Emily reached toward an overhead cupboard and pulled out eight mugs, placing them on the counter top ready for filling.

He watched as she carefully filled each one ready for distribution to the house guests. "You've got a system, haven't you?"

She grinned at him. "I do, and it works."

"My brother is a baker – he works in the same way. He says it's more efficient, but I often wonder if there's more to it."

She laughed and the sound sent a thrill down his spine. He stiffened.

"Once you learn what works best, you stick to it. Finding it can take time though."

He didn't trust himself to speak, and nodded.

"I watched my mother do all this," she indicated with her hands, "For many years. I basically followed in her footsteps."

She finished filling the mugs and he reached for them. "Leave them," she said abruptly. "You're going to end up with a bad reputation. I saw the reaction you got from the other men. You don't want repercussions."

Emily stared at him, daring him to disagree.

But he could outstare the best of them. "I don't care what they think," he said gently. "Let me help."

She nodded then reached for a tray and loaded the filled mugs onto them. All except two that wouldn't fit. "It's too heavy for me, so perhaps you wouldn't mind carrying it?"

"Of course."

He picked it up and could see why she wouldn't be able to carry it. She was a petite woman, and stood far below his shoulder. The weight would be far too much for her.

He carried the beverages into the sitting room where the men had retired. He was beginning to see what was going on here. Emily was being treated like a slave.

They had collectively decided if they paid rent, they didn't have to do anything. He would like to see that change.

Emily carried their mugs into the dining room. He totally understood her reasoning – the further away from these fools the better as far as he was concerned.

He stared over his mug at her, only to discover she was studying him too. So far he liked Grand Falls. It wasn't tiny but wasn't overly big either. The work he would do with *Sawdust Harry* would change all that.

"How long are you staying?"

Her words startled him out of his thoughts and he shook himself. "No idea at this point." Hopefully a very long time. He already had feelings for Emily and he'd known her for less than twenty-four hours. How would he feel after a few weeks?

She looked deflated.

"Definitely long enough to fix those cupboards, and probably long enough to do more." If Harry Johnson had been truthful, there was enough work to last for nearly a year, possibly longer.

The noise coming from the sitting room was becoming distracting. "Would you like to go for a stroll?" She frowned, but a smile formed on her lips. "We don't have to if you don't…"

She interrupted him. "I do, but worry about that lot."

He stood and took her empty mug from her hands and headed toward the kitchen. "I'm sure they'll cope." Then a thought struck him. "How often do you get time for yourself?"

As she leaned against the kitchen counter she stared at the floor. "Not often." Her words were soft, and he could hear the guilt creep into them.

He rinsed their mugs, then reached for her hand. "That changes now." Patrick saw the light spark in her eyes, and knew this was exactly what she needed.

There was a chill in the air at night, she told him, then went to her private lodgings to get her coat. He did the same.

While he waited in the foyer he listened to the raucous laughter of the other lodgers. Despite having met them only briefly, he knew them.

He'd met their sort before – treated women like slaves. He was certain that was happening here. Patrick had studied them as their food was placed in front of them, seen how they glared at him when he helped.

They were more than worried he would set a precedence and their easy lives would change. He certainly hoped that happened, and sooner rather than later. Emily looked exhausted.

Caring for seven grown men shouldn't be that hard, that demanding, but this lot had made it so.

He stared as she came slowly down the stairs. She'd fixed her hair. Not that it had needed fixing, but she'd let it down.

It suited her. He moved toward her as she was almost at the bottom of the stairs and held out his arm to her to take.

"You look lovely," he said quietly.

She patted her hair. "Thank you," she whispered, averting her eyes. Had she not been complimented before? That would be a terrible shame – she was a beautiful woman who needed to be praised.

She pulled on her gloves as they went outside, and Patrick did the same. He'd lived in Montana all his life, but he still couldn't get used to the bone-chilling night air.

She led him down the alleyway they'd traveled down earlier today, except now it was dark and eerie. "I won't walk along here alone at night," she said, glancing across at him. "Not that we have a lot of crime here.

He held her hand tighter, and she glanced at him again. "Thank you for taking me out. Sometimes that lot gets to me."

Patrick could totally understand that. "Do they ever give you trouble?"

She chewed on her bottom lip, and turned her head away. "Not really," she said quietly.

He could feel anger building inside him. "What does that mean?" He could feel himself tensing, and was certain she could feel it too.

"You saw them. They are a lazy lot. At least they'll be gone soon and a new bunch will come in." She brushed back a stray piece of hair, and he desperately wanted to do the same.

They came to the end of the alleyway and headed toward the main road where they walked along the wooden sideboard.

Emily pointed out some of the businesses along the main road. "This is the Saw Mill office. I'm guessing you'll have dealings with Daniel Carson who owns the saw mill."

They moved along to the next shop. "You've seen the Mercantile. Over there is the diner, then we have the dressmaker, and the bank. The doctor's office is out of town a little, but not far."

As she continued to point out the businesses, Patrick had lost interest. Not that he didn't want to learn about the town, but he'd prefer to learn about Emily Stanton.

She was much more interesting.

They stood side by side at the railing and he looked about. He could definitely see himself living here long-term. Especially if Emily was part of the deal.

He had never before felt drawn to a woman, and had not understood how his brother had been smitten with his mail-order bride after such a short time.

He was beginning to understand.

"Is there any night-life here?" he asked. Not that he went out much – there hadn't been much time for that.

"Only if you like to have a drink. The Commercial is a little further down the road. You can see the lights if you stare hard enough."

He wasn't interested. He'd seen enough men who couldn't hold their liquor, who'd taken it out on their wives. Most had drank away their food money. Patrick wasn't into that.

He worked hard for a living and would spend his money wisely.

"I'm not interested," he said gently. "I'd rather stay at home and have an interesting conversation with someone I care about."

She stared at him. "Except there is no one in Grand Falls you care about. Is there?"

He grimaced and she averted her eyes. "As it happens, there is," he said firmly. "I really don't know you Emily Stanton, but I don't like the way you are being treated."

She waved a hand in the air. "Don't worry about them. I can handle even the most vile of men." She stiffened and it made him wonder.

Had she been accosted by one of her lodgers? He certainly hoped not.

"We should go back," she said, hooking her arm through his again. "It's been nice to get out, but I still have some cleaning up to do."

He nodded. What else could he do? The last thing he wanted to do was make Emily's life more difficult.

Starting tomorrow, he would do whatever he could to make it easier for her.

* * *

Emily's eyes fluttered open at the crack of dawn. Sunlight filtered through the too-thin curtains, and she stretched herself out to her full length.

She slowly slid to the side of the bed, her feet hitting the cold floor. It made her wake up quickly.

She'd moved the rug from the bedside to ensure she did exactly that. Otherwise, she walked around in a haze for far too long.

She made her way to the converted bathroom where she had indoor plumbing. It cost a whole two months rent, but it was worth the expense. She'd had the men's bathroom converted at the same time which had saved quite a bit of money.

It had really gone against the grain to waste precious money on such an indulgence, but she had never regretted it.

Emily stared at herself in the bathroom mirror. She'd slept better last night than she had for ages. Perhaps it was the fresh air from her walk last night.

Her walk with Patrick…

She shook herself and tried to keep in mind he was just passing through. For sure Patrick wouldn't be here long. As soon as he was settled, he would find permanent accommodation and she would never see him again.

The thought made her miserable.

Emily had never been interested in men. She'd never had the time, and besides, she'd never met a man who caught her attention.

Patrick was different. He was well spoken, helpful, and…her heart skipped a beat when he was near.

She sucked in a breath.

She was not interested in Patrick Harper, and more likely than not, he was far from interested in her.

She would keep telling herself until she was convinced.

She splashed cold water on her face and dried it off, then pulled on her undergarments and a house-dress. Catching a glimpse of it in the mirror, Emily decided she needed to revamp her wardrobe. This gown was more than a little threadbare. Her remaining gowns were even worse.

She stared at her reflection. Why would she worry about that now? She'd never bothered before.

It was right there, in the back of her mind – Patrick Harper was the reason why. She wanted to look her best for him.

She stiffened.

She'd give him a week, and guaranteed, he'd be gone. Sawdust Harry would set him up somewhere else. Probably somewhere closer to wherever they were working.

Emily snatched up her keys and opened the door to her private accommodation. When her grandfather had decided to set up the boarding house, he'd ensured his family's privacy by setting up what amounted to an apartment.

If you didn't know better, it could be seen as a family home. There was a kitchen, bathroom, sitting room, and three bedrooms, with the master bedroom far larger than the other two rooms.

As it had turned out, by the time her father had taken over the business, she was the only child, so one room stood empty.

Father wanted to utilize the room further and rent it out, but Mother would have none of it. Emily had heard them argue over it several times.

If he had his way, Mother said it would put Emily in both moral and physical danger. She hadn't understood it at the time, but she certainly did now.

She was more than a little relieved her mother had stood up for her.

As she slowly went downstairs, Emily reveled in the quiet that surrounded the house. Most of the men would still be sleeping, but it wouldn't be long and they'd be up and demanding breakfast.

She sighed. The business had become a burden she no longer wanted to bear but it was too late now. She had no choice in the matter. Unless she decided to sell. There were no other heirs to the business, so that was an option worth exploring.

She groaned softly. Father would be turning over in his grave. On the other hand, Mother would be applauding her.

As she stood in the doorway to the kitchen, Emily heard muffled sounds behind her and turned, then gasped.

"Oh! It's you Mr Jasper." She put her hands to her chest. "You startled me." She turned back to enter the kitchen. "I'll put the kettle on and you can have a coffee if you'd like."

"What I'd like, Missy, is you." He lunged toward her and leered. Emily found herself pushed up against the center counter.

Her hands went up and she pushed against him, but the man was far bigger than her, and strong. Really strong.

"Stand back and get your hands off the lady." Patrick's voice rang out loud and clear through the room.

Where had he come from?

He moved around the counter and stood next to her assailant. She glanced across long enough to see the anger on his face. Aaron Jasper hadn't moved, not one inch.

"Last chance." Patrick stretched to his full height and towered above the man pinning her to the counter. His hand suddenly landed on Aaron's shoulder, and he pulled the man backwards and away from her.

Emily's heart pounded. She felt light-headed and downright terrified.

She stood helplessly watching as Patrick marched the man roughly into the sitting room. She stared as he pushed him into a chair then spoke to him.

No, that was untrue. Patrick lectured him. His body language told her everything.

By the time he returned to the kitchen, Emily had her heart rate under control, and the kettle was near boiling.

She stood at the counter facing the doorway. The last thing she needed was for someone to creep up on her again.

He stared at her, then came to stand beside her, his hand resting gently on her shoulder. "Are you alright?"

She nodded, not trusting herself to speak.

Emily glanced up at him – what she really wanted to do right now was to lean into him, to feel his comforting arms around her. But that wouldn't do. She was a strong woman, she'd proved that time and time again.

She would not let down her defenses over such a silly incident.

So instead she moved to the cupboard and pulled out two mugs, ready for coffee. As she turned, she discovered the reason he'd been in the kitchen, out of sight.

Spread across the floor, on the other side of the counter was a variety of tools – hammer, screwdrivers and a saw. One of the cupboard doors lay haphazardly on the floor.

She stared at it, not making sense of anything.

"What…" She couldn't comprehend the situation but knew something was wrong. The sound of crockery hitting the floor had her even more confused.

She stared down at the shattered mess. Gentle hands held hers and led her out of her former safe place. Everything was a blur and she was barely registering what was going on.

"Sit here." He squatted in front of her and studied her face. "I'll be back shortly" His voice seemed to be coming from a distance, yet he was right in front of her.

It seemed like forever before he returned, pushing a mug of tea toward her. "Miss Stanton? Emily?" He watched her every move. "Drink this."

She reached out and took the proffered beverage. It tasted good, sweet. She stared at him over the rim of the mug.

"You've had a nasty shock," he said quietly. "The tea will help." He squatted down in front of her again, and ensured she drank every drop.

He was right, she did feel better, but the reality of what happened was finally sinking in. She could feel tears brimming in her eyes, and she fought with all her might, until finally she let them run free.

Patrick Harper pulled her close and let her cry on his shoulder. What was it about this man that made her feel vulnerable and special all at the same time?

Chapter Three

Patrick began to prepare breakfast, but Emily couldn't let him do it alone.

He'd been amazing. No one had ever stood up for her like that before. But then, she'd never been accosted like that before.

She'd had a few of the gents make lewd comments and she'd brushed them aside. But none had ever become physical with her – until now.

Would it happen again? She shivered.

"I can manage if you want to rest." He studied her until she pulled her gaze away. "I can make a hot meal with the best of them." His grin lit up his face, and it made her feel better.

He'd pulled the mugs down from the cupboard and placed them on the center counter for her. Probably didn't want a repeat of earlier. The mugs had shattered beyond recognition, and Patrick had kindly cleared away the mess.

She reached for her apron and began to tie it behind her back. "Here, let me." His gentle voice matched his gentle touch, and Emily's heart thudded in her chest.

She glanced at him over her shoulder. "Thank you. It's been a difficult day." She closed her eyes tight. If she let them, her tears would flow again.

Emily had never been a crier, but this morning's episode had left her petrified. How would she cope with Aaron Jasper living here?

His hands cupped her shoulders and her pulled her back against him. She molded into him. "Just so you know, Mr Jasper is leaving right after breakfast."

"But…"

"You're not safe with him around. I'll willingly pay his next week's rent."

She spun around to face him. "Seriously?" Money wasn't the issue here, it was the gesture. No one had ever stood up for her before, nor had they made such a generous offer.

"Seriously." He reached into his pocket and pulled out some notes, but she pushed his hands away.

She looked him up and down. What kind of man was this who stood before her? Most of her lodgers kept their distance. They barely spoke a word, and the main time she saw them was when they were in the dining room eating.

It was a good arrangement, and one she reveled in. That way she had no attachment to any of them.

But this lodger was different. Patrick Harper was different. He was a true gentleman, and she could easily get used to him.

"If you make the toast, I'll cook the bacon and eggs." He already had the pan heating, and she threw in enough bacon for everyone. She reached for the skillet and put that on to heat as well.

She glanced across to see Patrick had the toast under control and had set out the plates ready for the food.

It felt as though she was under scrutiny as she cracked more than a dozen eggs into the skillet. By the time the food was cooked, Patrick had all the toast buttered, and the coffees made.

"You've done this before?" She was taken aback. Not many men were skilled in the kitchen.

A small smile crossed his face. "My father was a baker and the whole family pitched in. I am not the best cook around, but I can get by."

She reached out and covered his hand with her own. "Thank you. You've been a tremendous help."

They loaded the tray with the filled plates, and Patrick carried them into the dining room. All eyes turned their way. Except for Aaron Jasper. He turned his head in the opposite direction as they entered the room.

She could feel anger filling her senses, and tried to damp it down. One look at Patrick and she felt better. He was there by her side, and would ensure she was safe.

But what was she to do when he left? There was no way to predict the behavior of her lodgers. That had been proven with Aaron Jasper. He'd been here for about two weeks, and not a peep from him.

Then suddenly…this.

Patrick placed food in front of the offending man, then positioned a heavy hand on his shoulder. Mr Jasper stared up at him. She watched as Patrick leaned in and whispered something. The man stared ahead and nodded.

It was then Emily caught a glimpse out the corner of her eye. His suitcase sat ready for him to pick it up and leave.

The coffees were distributed and the pair took their place at the table. Patrick led the prayer of thanks, and included Emily in his words. It made her feel somewhat comforted.

She had prayed for help for such a long time, and finally her prayers had been answered.

* * *

Measurements in hand and Emily by his side, Patrick headed for the saw mill office. He would eventually be working with the owner, so why not introduce himself now?

He glanced across at the frail-looking woman by his side. It was apparent she was still shaken by the mornings event.

He was still fuming at the actions of that monster. Patrick had never come so close to hitting another man.

Rage burned inside of him. Aaron Jasper was lucky he hadn't been thrown out at that very moment. Or reported to the sheriff. He'd pleaded with Patrick to at least let him gather his possessions.

He'd suddenly felt bad for the man, but not bad enough to risk another attack on Emily.

He stole a quick glance and noticed her features had softened. He reached up and patted her hand.

She had balked at venturing out when she had so much to do, but admitted to enjoying their stroll the previous night. Besides, she did need to visit the Mercantile today.

"This is it," she said quietly. They went inside and waited for assistance.

The Saw Mill owner, Daniel Carson, introduced himself and was more than happy to meet them both. He noted the measurements and promised to deliver the order by the end of the week.

He would supply the timber at a good price, since they could mostly use offcuts from other timber orders they fulfilled during the week. A perk resulting from Patrick being the new carpenter in town.

They stepped outside and headed toward the Mercantile. They ambled along the walkway in silence.

Patrick had never been one for the ladies – he'd been more focused on his career. Besides, he'd never met anyone that interested him.

That changed the moment he met Emily Stanton. There was something about her that drew him in.

He leaned into her.

The lavender water she wore permeated his senses. But that wasn't the thing that drew him to her. He wasn't really certain what it was.

He stared at the businesses across the road. "Why don't we indulge ourselves?" He pointed toward the diner that stood out above all the other buildings.

She turned to him and smiled. "That would be nice. I haven't been there for such a long time."

They crossed the dirt road and headed toward the building. The word "Diner" was painted in big red letters across the large glass panel. Underneath, in smaller letters, it said "Proprietor: E. Baker".

Patrick opened the door for her and they were greeted by an older woman. "Good morning, Emily," she said warmly, then glanced across at Patrick.

"Who is this handsome young man?" She raised her eyebrows quizzically.

Emily giggled. "Mrs Baker, let me introduce Mr Patrick Harper." The older woman reached out her hand to him. "He's going to work with Sawdust Harry."

Mrs Baker pursed her lips. "Poor Harry. He is such a gentleman, and to be nicknamed in such a way…" She shuddered.

Emily giggled again. He was beginning to enjoy the sound of her laughter.

"A table for two?" Instead of waiting for an answer, they were led to a table near the fireplace. Not that the fire was going, because it wasn't.

He glanced across at it curiously. Why take them there specifically?

She must have read his mind because Mrs Baker suddenly said, "I thought it would be quieter for you here."

He looked about – they were the only customers. "It won't be long and the luncheon crowd will arrive."

Before he could question her further, Mrs Baker was gone.

She returned a short time later with two menus. Emily waved it away. "Just a coffee for me please, Mrs Baker."

He glanced across at the far-too-thin woman sitting opposite him. "Two coffees and… do you have cake?"

"Today we have carrot cake and blueberry muffins."

He glanced across at Emily. She shook her head. "Two slices of carrot cake please."

A small smile graced the lips of Mrs Baker moments before she left. He could see she was going to be supportive when needed. And frankly, it didn't bother him.

Emily was decidedly thin – it seemed apparent she'd run herself ragged in that boarding house. The main reason, from what he'd observed in the short time he'd been there, was the reluctance of the other lodgers to help out.

For the measly few dollars they were paying each week, they expected to make a slave of her. They would pay far more to rent a house!

Indignancy washed over him. How dare those men expect more of Emily than she was capable of doing.

He glanced across as he felt her soft, warm hand slip over his work-roughened hand. "You look upset." She squeezed his hand, and it sent tingles running through his veins.

Patrick stiffened. The whole situation angered him. "It's those lodgers. They treat you like a slave."

She patted his hand. "It's fine. Please don't worry."

Mrs Baker arrived with a tray of food and beverages before he could say what he truly felt.

Emily glanced up at her. "Thank you," she said quietly.

The older woman grinned at her. "I expect you to eat every crumb of that cake. Patrick is right – you are far too thin."

"I didn't…" Did he? He didn't think he'd said the words out loud.

She tapped her temple with her fingers. "I'm a mind-reader from way back." She grinned as she picked up the tray and disappeared again.

Emily took a sip of her coffee and stared at him over the rim of her cup. "I'm not you know," she said, taking another sip.

He shook his head in confusion. "You're not what?"

"Too thin." She put the cup down onto the saucer and wiped her tempting lips with the linen napkin next to her. She lifted an arm to show him. "I'm thin-boned. Mother always said I was." She lifted the cup to her lips again.

He reached out to touch her arm. He knew he shouldn't, but did it anyway. Before his hand connected, she pulled her arm away. Was she hiding something, or was she simply acting according to social propriety?

As she stared at him, Patrick tried to ignore his thundering heart. He'd never felt so smitten with a woman before, and he sure as heck didn't want to now.

He'd come here to do a job. And that was to build houses and stores to expand this great city.

That's exactly what he would do. In the meantime he would have as little to do with Emily Stanton as possible.

Only it was too late. She had already made her way into his very being. And into his heart.

He was beginning to understand how his brother, Ethan, had become so enamored with his new wife, despite only having known her for a matter of days.

"Eat your cake," he said gently. It might only be cake, but she needed nourishment to build her up. He wondered if she'd been skipping meals in order to care for her selfish lodgers.

He certainly hoped not.

When they finished their refreshments, she was keen to leave. "I have a lot to do," she said firmly as they stood. "Do you mind if we call to the Mercantile?"

He didn't. After all, they were heading there when he'd spotted the diner. After paying the bill, he accompanied her to the store. He looked about while she got her few supplies. He glanced up in time to notice her picking out a new gown.

"That color will look good on you," he said, his eyes roaming the lilac gingham gown. He spotted a matching bonnet and snatched it up. She frowned. "My gift to you," he said gently.

She still frowned. "Then I shall leave the gown."

"Then I shall buy the gown as well."

She fairly glared at him.

He laughed. "So what shall it be, Miss Stanton?"

She snatched up the gown in annoyance and headed to the counter with the gown and two loaves of fresh bread for luncheon. Patrick followed but she demanded the bonnet be added to her account.

Chapter Four

The nerve of the man! How dare he call her too thin. And how dare he try to buy her gifts without her permission.

Her arm reluctantly linked through his, she walked stiffly back home.

He glanced across and patted her hand. "You're not still mad at me, are you?" He grinned as he said the words.

She glared at him. "Yes." It came out much more forceful than she'd intended, but at least it would get her point across.

"Dear Miss Stanton," he said, patting her hand again like she was a dog that needed consoling. "I don't know why you have such an issue with me wanting to buy you an inexpensive gift." He frowned at her. "I truly love that color gown you bought. It brings out the color in your eyes."

She pursed her lips. "I doubt it – my eyes are brown."

"Then perhaps it was the color of your skin." This time he unabashedly grinned.

He looked down at the brown paper bag holding the despised item. "It is really such a bad thing that I wanted to buy a small gift for you?"

Patrick looked truly confused. And annoyed.

He honestly didn't know?

"It is what it represents that is the problem," she said harshly.

"I don't understand." They stood at the edge of the walkway before turning onto the alleyway.

She swallowed before answering. "What you might…expect of me in exchange for the gift." She refused to look into his face, and turned her head away. She felt the heat creep into her cheeks.

"Oh my Lord," he said, obviously distressed. "It means nothing of the sort." He paced the street, back and forth, until she reached out and grabbed his arm. "Is that what you think?"

He looked hurt, and pain crossed his features.

She shook her head. "You're not like that. But others may not see it that way." She opened the bag and glanced inside. "It is a lovely bonnet though." She smiled hesitantly.

He reached into his pocket and pulled out enough coins to cover the cost of the contentious item. Patrick dropped them into the bag.

She pursed her lips again.

"No-one knows but us two. And I promise, I expect *nothing* of you." He looped his arm through hers once more, and before she had a chance to protest, he lead her toward home.

Emily headed straight for the kitchen where she deposited the loaves of bread.

Patrick followed her. "I'll put this door back where it belongs so it's not in your way," he said, lifting the cupboard door from the counter top.

She nodded then left the room to put the gown away. As she opened the wardrobe door to hang it up she squealed. The rickety door almost fell off its hinges. It had been a problem before, but this time it looked to be beyond redemption.

Would Patrick mind fixing it for her? Probably not, but could she risk having him in her private quarters?

It was a question she would have to ponder.

She slipped into the bathroom where she freshened up. Emily stared at herself in the mirror. She traced the edges of her face.

Despite her anger of this morning, she looked more relaxed.

Patrick Harper had done that to her. She really liked him, but what about her rule? The *'no relationship with lodgers'* rule?

She shook herself as she continued to stare. Who was she trying to fool? They didn't have a relationship – they'd only just met.

"You're an idiot," she said under her breath, then walked away.

* * *

The men had all piled into the dining room, waiting for their luncheon. Most of them had worked in the morning, and would have recently arrived home according to Emily.

They sat around the table and stared at Patrick who stood then glanced across at Emily. "There are going to be some changes," he said firmly.

There were faint mumbles.

"As of today, you will get your own sandwiches. Miss Stanton will lay out the fillings in the kitchen and you will help yourself."

The murmurs got louder. "The same will apply to those of you who take a cut lunch during the week."

"What!"

"You can't do that!"

Patrick spoke again, but had to talk louder this time. "You will also pour your own coffee at each meal."

"We pay for that service!"

"You just got here. Who made you boss?"

Patrick put his hand up to stop the complaints. "Take a good look at Miss Stanton. She is unwell – you have all run her into the ground. If you don't stop treating her like a slave, there will be no lodgings available."

They all stopped dead in their tracks knowing they'd be in a dire situation without this boarding house and its beyond low rent. One, then another man pushed back his chair and headed toward the kitchen without another word of complaint. The others followed.

Patrick trailed them, grabbing Emily's hand and taking her with him. "One at a time. And don't be pigs," he said. "There's plenty of food."

They all knew Aaron Jasper had been evicted that morning, so perhaps they were being on their best behavior. The problem was, how long would it last?

He wouldn't be there forever, and what would happen when he left? He felt sure that without his insistence, the lodgers would all go back to their old habits.

Each man made his sandwich, then poured his coffee without complaint and returned to the table.

"You're a miracle worker," Emily said quietly as she made her sandwich. "I've been trying to implement this for ages. They wouldn't comply."

"They will now," Patrick said firmly. "I'll be here to make sure they do." He grabbed two coffee mugs and poured both their beverages, then made his own food.

Emily cut up a pound cake ready for the men when they finished their luncheon. They picked up their food and drinks and headed to the dining room.

Patrick felt a great sense of achievement. It seemed this had been a long time coming. Emily needed a reprieve from the constant and relentless work she was doing, otherwise she would soon collapse in a heap.

And that was the last thing he wanted to happen to her.

When they'd all finished eating, one of the older men – his name was George if Patrick recalled correctly – spoke to him. "What else can we do to help?" he asked firmly, glancing around the table.

Patrick put his mug down, surprised at the question. "From now on, all meals will be served to the counter in the kitchen, and each of you will collect your food from there."

He looked around the table. Not one man objected. He turned to Emily. "Are there other ways we can help?"

She chewed her bottom lip as she thought. "It would be a big help if each man made his own bed in the morning."

Patrick shoved his chair back and stood, glaring at them all. "You lot should be ashamed of yourselves. I have made my own bed since I was five years old. From now on you make your own beds every day."

They nodded their acquiesce, and Patrick continued. "I expect everyone to do their bit. Take a long hard look at Miss Stanton. She is skin and bone, and it cannot continue." He glanced around the table. "If you want to remain living here, things must change."

Satisfied the message had gotten through, he picked up his empty plate and headed to the kitchen. "Anyone want cake?" he asked over his shoulder, and every man followed him. He glanced back to see a satisfied smile on Emily's face.

* * *

Emily pulled on her new lilac gingham dress, then the matching bonnet Patrick had bought for her. She would feel so proud going to church today in her new outfit.

She stared at herself in the mirror – she looked very pretty, if she did say so herself. She pulled the bonnet off for now, and snatched up her white gloves and reticule, then headed out of her private apartment.

As she descended the stairs, she shoved the gloves into her reticule. Glancing down, she spotted Patrick in the foyer. He did look a treat in his Sunday best, and her heart did a little flutter.

He looked up and beamed at her. "I must say you look like perfection itself, Miss Stanton." He took a few steps toward her and her heart danced a little jig.

What was it about this man that made her heart happy?

She hesitated on the stairs. "It's too quiet. Where is everyone?" Normally at this time on a Sunday, most of the men were hovering around noisily, waiting to be fed.

"They each made their breakfast, and believe it or not…" He stepped closer and whispered. "George made a pot of coffee." He raised his eyebrows.

She was as surprised as Patrick.

"Do we have time for a quick breakfast before heading off?" He glanced down at his pocket watch. It was obviously a rhetorical question since he answered himself. "It looks as though we do."

He headed for the kitchen and she followed. Bacon, eggs, and toast were in the warmer of the wood stove, mugs were on the counter.

She stopped in her tracks. "You *are* marvelous," she said, a catch in her voice.

He shrugged his shoulders. "We have to fatten you up somehow." He stood grinning at her, and she fought back tears. Since her parents had died, Emily had been totally alone, and had run this boarding house entirely without help.

She had run herself ragged, as Patrick had surmised, and now here he was – her guardian angel, standing before her.

Protecting Emily from herself.

"I honestly don't know what to say," she said softly.

"Nothing to say," he said as he dished out their food. "You pour the coffee and I'll carry our food out to the dining room.

They had not long finished taking their soiled plates to the kitchen, when voices alerted her to the men waiting in the foyer. She quickly washed their dishes, then headed out to meet them.

"You look very pretty today, Miss Stanton," Abner Jameson told her. His words shocked her as he'd never given her a compliment before.

"I could say the same about you, Mr Jameson," she said gently.

Patrick pushed forward and offered her his arm, and Emily snatched up her bonnet as they left the house.

The other men scowled at him. Emily wondered how long it would take for them to object to her friendship with the newcomer. Especially since he was the one to implement new, more restricting rules for them.

They began as a group, but most of the lodgers walked at a quicker pace and arrived at the church ahead of the pair.

"Do you think they're annoyed?" Patrick glanced across as he asked the question.

She took her time answering. "Perhaps, but it had to happen. I cannot continue like this." She knew it was true, and was more than grateful for Patrick's intervention.

He nodded but didn't answer.

As they rounded the corner, the church stood proudly before them. Emily was nearly always overcome with emotion as she approached the church – this was the place her parent's funeral had been conducted. It held a lot of good memories, but the bad ones seemed to overshadow those.

They entered the building and they could hear organ music belting out the tune of *Onward Christian Soldiers*.

Most people had already taken their seats, including the gents from the boarding house. Emily guided Patrick to a seat at the back of the room since Preacher Angus Devon was already entering the room. Less disruption that way.

"Thank you everyone for coming today," he began. "It is always gratifying to see our humble building filled with believers." He smiled and looked about the room. "Let us bow our heads in prayer."

After the prayer, they went straight into another hymn. Emily reached for the hymn book at the same time Patrick did, and the contact sent a thrill rushing up her arm. She nearly dropped the book.

Patrick glanced curiously at her. Thank goodness he didn't realize the reason.

They all recited The Lord's Prayer at the end, then piled out of their seats once the preacher was in place at the entrance.

"Good morning, Preacher Devon," Emily said. "I'd like to introduce Mr Patrick Harper. He is new to Grand Falls."

"Welcome to our church family," the preacher said as he offered his hand. "Are you staying or just passing through?"

Patrick didn't hesitate. "I hope to be here for some time. I've come to help Harry Johnson with the housing growth."

"Ah, another carpenter. Exactly what this town needs, eh, Miss Stanton."

She smiled. "He's already helping me around the boarding house," she said. "It is truly wonderful having another crafty man in town."

They said their goodbyes then moved outside. Emily liked to stay for coffee and biscuits, but she wasn't so sure today. She would prefer to leave now, and have Patrick all to herself. She'd been enjoying their strolls of late, enjoyed having his full attention.

"Are you coming, Emily?" It was Mrs Baker from the diner. She glanced at Patrick and grinned. "I see you have your young man with you."

Emily opened her mouth to object, but Patrick laughed, distracting her. "Coming where?" he asked, totally oblivious to their after church ritual.

Mrs Baker walked over and hooked her arm through Patrick's. Then they strolled toward the hall as Mrs Baker explained about their morning beverages.

A pang of something stung her heart. Surely not jealousy? Mrs Baker was old enough to be Patrick's mother. She straightened her shoulders and followed the mis-matched pair into the hall.

Chapter Five

Morning coffee at the church had been good.

Patrick met up with a few people he was already acquainted with – Daniel Carson from the Saw Mill, Cecil Delbert from the Mercantile, and of course Mrs Baker.

He also met people he'd not encountered before and his head was spinning with all the names and faces. Not being particularly good with names, he wouldn't remember them all. Not yet anyway.

As an added bonus, Harry Johnson was also there. He seemed like a friendly chap, and Patrick quickly warmed to him.

Harry was currently working on a cottage which wasn't far from Emily's boarding house. From what he'd learned today, the town had quickly grown once the railway had arrived. Not that anyone was complaining – business in Grand Falls was booming.

Prior to the fairly recent arrival of the railway they'd had to travel to Fort Benton, which Emily said had taken her grandfather three days by buckboard to visit the Trading Post near there.

Life was certainly difficult back then, but he was pleased Emily didn't have to endure that lifestyle.

He was ready for the hard work ahead, after all, this was what he'd trained for and dreamed of all his adult life.

Building his brother's bakery and home in Dayton Falls had been one of the best decisions Patrick had made for a long time. It meant he could use them as examples of his recent work.

Sending photographs had been even better.

He glanced across and noticed Emily fidgeting. *Did she want to leave?*

Patrick pulled out his pocket watch. Good grief – it was after noon. She would be itching to prepare luncheon for the lodgers.

Despite Sunday being the day of Our Lord and a day of rest, there was no rest for Emily. She seemed to be on the go seven days a week. At least now the pressure had been eased a little.

He would try to entice her into a stroll again this afternoon. Perhaps he could even hire a horse and buggy from the livery and take her for a drive in the countryside.

He was thoughtful – that would be quite pleasant on such a lovely Spring day. What a pity he hadn't planned ahead; he could have made it a picnic outing.

Perhaps next time.

As they headed back home, Emily linked her arm through his. She didn't look quite so agitated now. They heard the murmur of voices as they entered the boarding house.

The aroma of the cooking roast was more than a little enticing. She had earlier told him her routine was to prepare the roast very early, before anyone else was awake. He was constantly amazed at her resilience.

She quickly ran upstairs to her private quarters to offload her bonnet and reticule, then returned without delay.

Emily reached for her ruffled apron and checked the food cooking in the oven. He watched mesmerized as she pulled the roast out of the oven and transferred everything to a platter.

Then she began to make the gravy using the juices from the food.

She reminded him so much of his mother. She had always tried to please everyone, and ran herself ragged doing so. Perhaps that is the reason he was determined to make Emily's life easier?

He didn't want her to have an early demise like his dear mother.

"What can I do to help?" She startled at his words, so intent was her concentration.

She turned to face him, her hand to her chest. "Perhaps set the plates out on the counter ready for serving?"

She reached into a low cupboard and pulled out two large gravy boats, while continuing to stir the gravy. "They belonged to my grandmother, and I treasure them greatly," she said quietly.

Patrick nodded. His mother had something similar, with pretty pink flowers on them, not unlike these.

He felt completely useless once he'd set the plates and mugs out on the counter. Emily said there was nothing more he could do, and began to dish out food. He carried the gravy boats to the dining room, then called the men to collect their food.

Surprisingly, not one protested, and collected their food and beverages without so much as a word of complaint.

Patrick's mouth was already watering.

Once everyone was seated, they joined hands and bowed their heads, then said a prayer of thanks.

Patrick felt a sense of renewal wash over him. This was a whole new life for him. He had a job that could last for anything from a few months to several years. But the way Harry Johnson spoke, if he did a good job, which he would, he could live the rest of his days here.

He thought about what he wanted from life. It had always been to find a permanent position as a carpenter. He now had that, and Patrick wondered what the next step in his life would be.

Until a few days ago, he'd never thought about marrying. Not even when his brother had married. The thought had never entered his mind. But now things had changed.

Emily had brought about that change to his way of thinking. But was she even interested? She'd not shown any indication she was even the slightest bit taken with him.

He glanced up to see Emily staring at him. How long had he sat there daydreaming? He cut his food and took a mouthful. It was absolute bliss. "This is wonderful, Miss Stanton," he said, and the other men joined in with their vote of thanks.

She seemed more relaxed as each day passed. Patrick was so glad he'd come to this particular place to stay, otherwise he would have never met the alluring Miss Emily Stanton.

* * *

Patrick had convinced Emily to take another stroll this afternoon. She was beginning to look forward to spending time with him, even though she knew she shouldn't. The *'no relationship'* rule popped into her mind once more.

She brushed it away.

Emily finished up the dishes, with his help, then prepared for their afternoon out. Next week would be different – Patrick began work tomorrow and he would be too exhausted to help.

She brushed that thought away too. She hated the thought of not spending time with Patrick.

There wasn't a lot to do around town, but they would check with the livery, and if a wagon was available, they'd hire it.

Her heart fluttered.

She hadn't felt this excited since Johnny Toogood kissed her behind the school shed in grade six. His family had left town soon after, and she'd always blamed that kiss as the reason. It had been years before she discovered his grandfather had died suddenly and left his thriving business to Johnny's father.

She hadn't thought about him for many years, and wondered why he'd popped into her head now. Was the promise of a kiss from Patrick making her imagination run wild?

Except Patrick hadn't promised her anything except a couple of hours of his time.

With the last of the dishes put away and the kitchen tidied up, Emily pulled off her apron and hung it up. "I'll go and get changed," she said over her shoulder as she left the kitchen.

Patrick reached out for her. "Why would you do that? You look so pretty today, Emily." He looked her up and down. "You look pretty every day, but the colors in your new gown really suit you."

She felt the color creep up her neck and cheeks. "Then I need to freshen up and grab my bonnet." She flashed him a smile and was on her way.

No matter what Patrick said to her, his words always made her feel better, and feel wanted. He was the sort of man that when he walked into a room, everyone noticed.

And everyone took notice of what he said.

From the moment they'd met, a sort of calmness had descended on her. What was it about Patrick Harper that made her feel that way?

Emily inwardly shook herself. She was thinking like a crazy woman. How could one man make all that happen?

Only it had. She'd seen it with her own eyes. He had stood at the end of the table and commanded the lodgers change their ways and they had. He was a born leader, and she loved that about him.

By the time she returned, Patrick had changed out of his suit and was waiting at the bottom of the stairs.

She hooked her arm in his, and they headed for the livery. Their expectation was low as Emily was certain it would be closed on a Sunday afternoon.

When they arrived chains were up, indicating the livery was closed. As they turned away, a young voice called to them. "Whatcha want?" the young boy said, as they faced him. "Pop ain't here today, but I can help."

Patrick grinned at the confident young man striding up to him. "We're looking to hire a horse and buggy for two or three hours," he said, reaching into his pocket.

The boy motioned for him to leave the money and to follow him. "What are you up to Charlie?" Emily asked the young boy.

He looked about suspiciously. "Follow me, an' I'll getcha wagon. Just don't tell me pop and I'll give it to ya cheap." His eyes lit up and Emily knew without a doubt the boy would pocket the money.

Not her concern.

Patrick pulled three notes out of his wallet once they were out of sight, and Charlie's eyes opened wide. The boy snatched up two of them. "Take all three," Patrick urged, but the boy would have none of it.

"Nah. If I have too much, Pop will get suspicious." He shoved the notes into his pocket with his grubby hands. "This'll do." He prepared the horse and wagon for them and removed the chains so they could leave. "Make sure you're back before five, or Pop will beat me until I'm black an' blue."

Emily glanced across at Patrick, and watched as he cringed. "I don't want you getting into trouble, boy."

"Just come back in time an' I'll be fine," he said, handing over the reins.

Patrick helped her up onto the wagon, before climbing up himself. His touch was strong, but gentle and it sent shivers through her entire body.

The seat of the wagon was padded, but it was narrow, forcing them to sit close. Emily's leg rubbed against Patrick's and a thrill went through her.

As much as she looked forward to their little journey around the hillside, she wondered if she should continue. Their closeness was making her feel things she'd never felt before.

The moment the chains were down, Patrick urged the horse forward. "Ya!" And they were off.

He paused at the gateway. "Which way, Miss Stanton? Is there somewhere particular you'd like to go?"

She straightened her bonnet and looked to the left where most of the township stood, then looked to the right, where no-one would spy them together. "To the right, I think," she said as she studied him. "There are some lovely spots along the Mississippi River where we could stop, or you could continue up into the mountains."

He grinned. "The Mississippi it is."

She wondered what had him sounding so happy.

* * *

"Oh, I could never…"

Emily glared at him, and in return Patrick stood there laughing.

All he had asked was she remove her boots and stockings and let her bare legs dangle in the water. Anyone would think he'd asked her to go skinny dipping.

The thought had him laughing again.

"Ooooh, your are incorrigible, Mr Harper."

He certainly hoped so.

Despite all her objections, Emily found a grassy area next to a tree and plonked herself down. She untied her laces, and once he'd turned his back, had removed her stockings.

He hadn't planned it this way, but once they'd arrived, it seemed like a good idea. He'd already removed his shoes and socks and placed them on the wagon.

He'd tied old Nellie to a bush, and she was happily lapping up the sun.

"You can turn around now," Emily told him. "Don't you breathe a word of this to a soul. It would ruin my reputation!"

Pink flooded her cheeks, and he wondered how many ways there were to make that happen. He liked the way it brightened her face – she was far too pale and looked deathly ill some days.

"You'll need to lift your skirts a little," he said sheepishly, glancing across at her. He waited for the explosion, but there was none.

Instead she gave him an equally sheepish grin.

They sat on the edge of the river where it was fairly shallow and let their legs dangle. "This is nice," she said, glancing across at him. "I've never done anything like this before." She grinned. "I think the fun comes from knowing it is totally inappropriate."

She raised her eyebrows in defiance.

He reached for her hand and squeezed it. He wondered what other fun things she'd never done. "Have you ever been on a date, Miss Stanton," he asked gently.

Her eyes opened in wonder. "Are you asking me out on a date, Mr Harper?"

Was he? He wasn't sure, but perhaps he should. "Yes, I think I am Miss Stanton." He stared at her expectantly.

"Then I shall expect you to ask me properly." She flashed him a cheeky grin, and it was then he realized there was far more to Miss Emily Stanton than he may ever know.

He licked his suddenly dry lips. "Miss Stanton…" he said gently, cupping her hands in his own. "Emily, will you accompany me to dinner this evening?"

She frowned. "I can't – I have to feed the lodgers."

Those blasted lodgers. They had her tied down. Well not any more – he would see to that. "They can make their own dinner. You provided them with a roast luncheon, so they're not going to starve."

She nodded. *Was that a nod of agreement or something else entirely?*

His heart thudded in his chest waiting for her answer.

"Well Mr Harper, Patrick," He loved the way his name rolled off her tongue. "I think perhaps the gents can have sandwiches for their supper tonight, and we shall go on a date."

He was so happy, he pulled her into his arms and held her tight. Before he realized what he was doing, his lips brushed across hers and he reveled in the taste.

She pushed him away. "What are you doing?" Emily jumped up from the riverbank, snatched up her shoes and stockings, and stormed back to the wagon.

He was confused. Wasn't that what she wanted? He'd felt a connection between them and today was certain she'd felt it too.

Patrick ran after her, meeting her at the wagon, where she was pulling her boots back on. He moved from one foot to the other, staring down at the ground like a lovestruck teenager. "I apologize if I was out of line, Emily," he said with a catch in his voice. "I really like you and thought you felt the same."

She looked up at him with a grin on her face. She reached out both her arms and pulled him to her. "I do like you," she said. "I guess I got a bit scared. No man has ever kissed me before."

He wrapped his arms around and whispered in her ear. "Then Grand Falls is full of fools." He reluctantly pushed out of her embrace and studied her face. "You are a beautiful, caring, and very special woman, Emily Stanton. I would like your permission to court you."

She stared down at the ground. "I have a rule about not having relationships with lodgers," she said quietly.

For a moment he stared at her, the shock of her words hitting him hard. Then reality hit. "We're not having a relationship – yet. But if that was going to stop us, I would move out."

She said not a word, and it worried him. "Of course, it's up to you. If you don't want to go out with me…"

"Oh, but I do," she said quickly. "I made that rule to appease the townsfolk after my parents died. There's a strong lock on the door to my private quarters too. For the exact same reason."

She lifted her arms and he stepped into her embrace again. He kissed her forehead, then her cheek, and finally their lips met.

Patrick didn't want to leave this place – not only was it peaceful, he had Emily to himself without some lodger interrupting his thoughts.

No, they would have to leave soon. Young Charlie's wellbeing was at stake, and he couldn't live with himself if the boy took a beating because of his selfishness.

Chapter Six

Emily was in the kitchen making preparations for the lodger's supper when Patrick arrived back. After dropping her off close to home, he returned the horse and wagon to young Charlie. Then he'd gone to the diner and booked a table for later that evening. He would strike while the iron was hot.

Mrs Baker was thrilled at the prospect of their courtship, and didn't hold back on saying so.

On arriving back at the boarding house he heard the muffled voices of the gents in the dining room, and headed straight there. He stood in the doorway contemplating whether or not to say the words he'd pondered all afternoon.

One hand against the frame, he stood tall, extending himself to his full height. "I have something to say," he said loudly, aiming to get their attention.

The groans were more than a little clear.

"I hereby declare that Miss Stanton and myself are officially courting." He stared at each man individually daring them to object.

None did.

"Tonight we are going to the diner. Miss Stanton is preparing your supper now."

Suddenly George jumped up and shook his hand. "Congratulations, Mr Harper. If you don't mind me saying so, Miss Stanton needs someone like you to look after her."

Patrick stared at the man. Was he for real, or was he joking with him?

"You do the right thing by her, or you'll have all of us to answer to."

Obviously he wasn't kidding. George sat down again and each man came up and shook his hand but said little. Did he detect a pang of jealousy amongst them?

Patrick was certain he would have a mutiny on his hands, but thankfully it wasn't to be.

He was alerted to Emily's presence when she rested her hand on his shoulder. "I'll be ready shortly." She turned to the lodgers. "Supper is set out on the counter. Help yourselves."

She began to turn away, but spun back to face them. "There's madeira cake on the counter as well. It's already cut."

Patrick's hand slipped up around her waist. "That's very kind of you, Emily. I'm sure the gents will enjoy their supper."

A tirade of thanks followed and he guided her out of the room, a trail of men heading for the kitchen.

"I need to freshen up a little, but I won't be long," she said as she headed for the stairs. "I should get changed."

Patrick frowned. She looked perfect to him. Perhaps her hair needed fixing, but nothing more. "Please yourself, but you look beautiful already."

She beamed at him and disappeared up the stairs. When she returned she looked a treat, as he knew she would. She'd obviously fixed her hair as it didn't look disheveled like it had earlier.

As he moved closer, the fragrance of lavender drifted into his senses. "You smell as beautiful as you look," he said quietly so no one else could hear.

She blushed deeply. Patrick was delighted to be learning all the ways to make color come to her cheeks, but realized that underneath she was still thin and pale.

He was on a mission to repair that problem.

Patrick pulled the pocket watch out of his vest. "We must away. Mrs Baker is expecting us shortly."

Emily hooked her arm through his, and they moved toward the front door.

The weather was typical Spring and it was a warm night. The sun was low down in the sky, and hopefully there would be enough moonlight for them to walk home by. "Thank you for doing this," Emily said quietly, breaking into his thoughts.

"You don't need to thank me," he said as he stared into her beautiful brown eyes. He hoped one day soon they would sparkle as they should, but right now the spark had turned to a flat, dull color.

He wondered when that had happened.

They were greeted at the door by the lady herself – Mrs Baker. She'd told him earlier she would reserve a quiet spot up the back for them, and that's exactly what she had done.

The diner was far busier tonight, and was already more than half full. Patrick was pleased he'd made a reservation. He had no intentions of disappointing Emily.

He held the chair for her, and Emily sat down daintily, then removed her bonnet. He liked it when she let her blonde hair dangle around her shoulders, but tonight it was up. Sadly it accentuated the thin lines of her face when it was pulled back so tightly.

Mrs Baker handed them both a menu. "Beef stew with biscuits is the special tonight," she said, and before they'd even read the menu, each of them decided on the stew. "We'll talk dessert later," she said with a wink, then went to prepare their order.

A waitress returned a short time later with a jug of water and two glasses.

"You have a big day tomorrow," Emily said, referring to Patrick's first day at his new job. "We mustn't stay late."

She placed her hands on the table in front of her, and Patrick slid a hand across to hers. "You're right, but we'll stay here as late as necessary. I want tonight to be special."

The moment their skin touched, a shiver went down his spine. He had no idea what that meant, except he knew he was falling in love with the remarkable Emily Stanton.

The rest of the night went by in a blur. Patrick was so enthralled with Emily that his heart did flip-flops throughout the evening and his attention was on her, and her alone.

As delicious as the food was, Emily was far more worthy of his attention.

The stroll home was by moonlight, as Patrick had predicted. They walked along the dimly lit wooden boardwalk of the main road until they came to the alleyway. There was even less lighting here, and Patrick decided to use it to his advantage.

They were not far along when he stopped and pulled Emily into his arms. "I'm falling in love with you, Emily," he whispered as he cradled her in his arms.

"We hardly know each other," she whispered back. "As much as I've tried to fight it, I feel the same way."

He put his fingers under her chin and enticed her head back to allow him access to her lips. "You are so beautiful, and incredibly special," he said against her lips.

They separated as the sound of laughter alerted them they weren't alone. Patrick looked up to see a group of teenagers on the other side of the street. "Blasted kids. They should be home in bed."

Emily laughed with that adorable tinkle he loved so much. "It's only a little after eight o'clock," she reminded him as she laughed.

"Still, good children should be at home this hour of the night."

He hooked his arm through hers, the moment lost, and they continued back to the boarding house. "Do you want me to go?" he asked out of the blue, staring ahead, not daring to look at her, afraid of the answer.

She stopped abruptly and he nearly pulled her over. "Go where?" She gently turned him to face her with her fingers. "Patrick? Where are you going?" She seemed totally confused.

"I thought perhaps I should move out since we are now officially courting."

She closed her eyes momentarily and he took the chance to study her worried face.

She suddenly opened them again and he was caught staring. "No, I don't think you need to do that." She started walking again – apparently the conversation had ended.

Patrick took his key and unlocked the front door. There were mutterings coming from the sitting room as the door opened, but the moment they looked inside, the mutterings stopped.

There were questions about their night out, and then Emily went upstairs to retire for the night. Since he was the one who'd enticed her out, Patrick cleaned the kitchen back to its normal pristine state.

At least Emily wouldn't have to worry about that in the morning. He retired soon after, since he'd be up early for his first day working with Harry Johnson.

It felt like he was floating on air. His night out with Emily Stanton had been one of his happiest times for as long as he could remember.

* * *

Patrick was bent over the kitchen cabinet of the cottage Harry had been working on for some time. He'd mostly finished the shell, and needed Patrick to start on the inside.

The owners wanted to move in as quickly as possible. They'd quoted four weeks, Harry had told them it would be at least six. But now, with help, it would be much sooner.

"It's hard work we're doing here, Patrick," Harry said. "Having seen the photographs you sent, I know you are more than capable."

"Thanks," Patrick said, trying not to be distracted from his work.

"Let's take a break," Harry declared. "I'm hungry."

They sat under the shade of a tree, the grass thick and green, and each opened their lunch pails. Patrick had no idea what was in his, as Emily had packed it for him despite their recent new rule about lodgers making their own cut lunches.

He pulled out a wrapped sandwich filled with ham and cheese. A small note fluttered to the ground and he reached for it.

Miss you already. He missed her too.

The note made him smile.

"What is it?" Harry asked curiously.

Patrick showed him, but felt heat creeping up his face.

"You hang onto that young lady – she's a gem if ever there was one."

He stared down into the note. "I know," he said quietly. "She's one in a million, and I don't intend to lose her."

For the rest of their break, they talked about the project, and what came after it. The next project was another cottage, Harry told him. It was not far from this one, and was slightly larger.

Patrick liked the idea of something different for variety.

Harry pulled out the drawings for their current cottage, and showed him what was needed for the rest of the project. Patrick studied the drawing, then packed up his lunch pail and went back to work.

It hadn't been terribly long since he'd finished his last job – his brother Ethan's bakery and home – but his back was aching. He'd soon get used to it again.

Ethan had been pretty laid back, and Patrick had been able to do the work at his own pace. All that changed now he was working with Harry who had time limits.

His thoughts moved to Emily. What would she be doing now? Was she resting like he'd suggested, or was she slowly killing herself despite the changes made to her routine. ?

Now that he wasn't there to see for himself, his worry deepened. There was nothing he could do but wait and see after he finished work tonight.

Patrick shook the thoughts away, and returned to work. He'd never been so distracted by a woman as he was by the delightful Miss Emily Stanton.

* * *

Almost a week passed, and thankfully the timber arrived earlier than anticipated. Patrick decided to start work immediately.

He enjoyed spending time with Emily, even if it was only while he worked and she cooked. The aroma permeating the kitchen was more than a little enticing.

"Tell me which cupboard is giving you the most trouble," he said, and Emily pointed it out. It was also the one she used the most, so he was glad to be able to make things easier for her.

She glanced across as he worked, and he found it more than a little distracting. Everything about Emily was distracting – in the nicest possible way.

"What are you making," he asked, trying to break the silence.

"An apple and cinnamon loaf for supper." She smiled at him and he felt as thought someone had gifted him a million dollars.

She slowly looked better than when he'd first arrived, and he put it down to her workload being lightened. He had ensured she ate better too, so that had to also be a factor.

"This is the original kitchen from grandfather's time," she told him. "Except for a few modern additions."

He had already surmised that much. The entire kitchen was in need of a refurbishment, but for now, new cupboard doors, and some repairs here and there would get her through.

The building was old, there was no doubt. Patrick wondered how Emily had even managed with it this long.

There was so much he could do around the place to help her, but she was already vocal about him "spending his precious personal time" fixing her kitchen doors.

The truth was, he was reveling in spending time with her. He didn't care if he gave up his "personal time" – any time with Emily was special.

She leaned down and handed him a mug of water. "Thanks," he said, accepting it gratefully. It was quite warm in the kitchen with the wood stove running full blast. As well as the oven, she also had a stew cooking on the stove top.

He glanced up to where she was adding ingredients to yet another bowl. Coming from a family of bakers and cooks he recognized a batch of biscuits before she even emptied the dough onto the counter.

His Emily was the best cook.

He hesitated. His Emily?

A smile came to his face. Since he was courting her, he truly could say say that. Every moment he spent with her was precious.

The lodgers had changed their ways and now appreciated all she had done for them, now treating her with the respect she deserved.

"This one is finished," Patrick said, standing up and stretching. "Which one is next?"

She stopped what she was doing and frowned. "You've done far too much already. I hate that you work hard all day, then come home and continue working."

This was a quick job compared to his daily workload. He'd already fixed her wardrobe door, and now this one cupboard door. He was more than ready to do more.

She looked truly unhappy, and he needed to remedy the situation. Patrick stepped forward and pulled her into his embrace.

"Emily," he whispered, "Helping you is not a hardship. In fact, it makes my heart happy." He leaned back and gazed into her face.

Her lips called out to him, and his head slowly came down, giving her the opportunity to pull back. He hoped she wouldn't, but he had to give her the choice.

She looked up at him with those big brown eyes, pleading with him to kiss her.

And that's exactly what he did.

Emily closed her eyes and waited for the contact, and he almost chuckled at the sight. She was so sweet, so very innocent, and he adored her for it.

His lips brushed gently across hers, and even with the slightest touch, a tingle went down his spine. Patrick pulled her closer and kissed her again, this time a little deeper. He shivered as her arms snaked around him, not wanting to break the connection but fully aware of everything they were both yet to do before supper.

"Ahem."

They quickly separated at the sound coming from the doorway.

"I wondered if I could set the table for you," George said sheepishly, giving Patrick a wink. "Ah, your back is covered in flour," he said, as he gathered up the cutlery.

Emily stared at her hands. "Oh, I'm so sorry. I forgot I was covered in flour and dough." She began to brush at his back.

Patrick wasn't bothered. He would just change his shirt. "I'm not sorry," he said cheekily, as he left the room to change.

Emily stared at him open-mouthed.

Chapter Seven

It had taken a couple of weeks, but the kitchen cupboards had all been replaced and were now working.

Much to her dismay, Patrick had busied himself with other repairs around the place. Bookshelves, chairs, and even the bathroom cupboard.

He was a Godsend in many ways, and Emily truly appreciated him being there, but she hated that all his spare time was taken up making repairs.

They had been courting for some weeks now, but Emily was concerned. Not about the fact they were courting, she was certain she was in love with the magnificent Patrick Harper.

Her concern lay in the future of the boarding house. It had been in her family for three generations – what plans did Patrick have if they did eventually marry?

She had to stay here to look after the boarding house and lodgers. Would he agree to that, or would he wholly object?

Her heart ached. These are things she should have discussed with him when he first asked permission to court her. But honestly, she hadn't thought that far ahead.

It was then she realized there was no promise of marriage. *Just because she was being courted did not mean Patrick intended to marry her.*

She sat at her dressing table brushing her hair. Fifty strokes every night before bed. It was a ritual she had been undertaking since she was a young girl, except back then her mother did the brushing.

Emily truly missed her mother, but knew it was this place that put her in an early grave. Her eyes filled with tears for the mother she dearly loved and would never see again.

She closed her eyes and prayed. Even in her grief she knew Mother was in a better place. She was always such a frail and sickly woman. Working herself to the bone had not helped.

It was in that moment she realized Patrick was right about her own state of health. She opened her eyes and stared at her reflection. She looked much more healthy now than she had when he arrived. She'd even filled out to the extent she should replace some of her gowns.

Oh, they still fit, but some were a tad tight. They were all threadbare except for her most recent purchase, the lilac gingham gown which Patrick adored on her.

She made a decision to replace her ailing wardrobe. Going by her past experience, having new clothes would also lift her spirits.

Emily finished brushing her hair then climbed into bed. She lay staring at the ceiling until her eyes fluttered closed and her dreams were filled with thoughts of Patrick Harper.

* * *

"Good morning, Mr Delbert," Emily said. She had perused the range of fabrics at the Mercantile and chosen a few she liked. "Do you have a copy of The Delineator?"

"Butterick's pattern catalog? I do indeed Miss Stanton, but unless I have your chosen pattern in stock, you could wait up to a month for it to arrive."

A month? Emily felt deflated. After the response she'd had from her recent new gown, she'd felt a whole lot better. Perhaps it was all in her head, but things seemed to be picking up.

Patrick had particularly liked her that gown, and she always felt really good around him. On second thought, that may not have had anything to do with the gown. She chuckled to herself.

"Flick through and let me know what patterns you'd like. I can check if I have them here already." He glanced across the room. "Or you can look for yourself. They're in the corner over there."

Emily went through the patterns currently available, the dust tickling her nose. Apparently they were not the most popular items in the store, which surprised her.

She pulled two patterns from the box, and chose three different fabrics, her favorite was white poplin with dainty lilac flowers. She would never have considered lilac in the past, but Patrick seemed to admire the color on her…

It had been quite a time since Emily had done any sewing, but she'd been very competent at the time. If she got into any strife, she could always call on Joe Harkley who was the local tailor. They went to school together, and surely he would help her.

Heck, maybe she should take the material and patterns straight to Joe and save herself the trouble.

Still undecided, she took her purchases to the counter, and Cecil Delbert added them to her account, along with the pretty lace she'd found tucked away in a corner of the store.

She clutched the paper bag and headed for home. She had to pass Joe's tailor shop on her way, and decided to pop in and say hello.

Joe's father was the original tailor, but had trained his son from a young age to eventually take over. Tragedy had struck some years earlier, and her friend became the sole proprietor.

"Emily! What are you doing here?" Joe asked. "It been a long time." He looked her up and down. "You've grown into a beautiful young woman."

He stepped toward her and pulled her into a friendly hug. "What brings you here?"

Emily hugged him back, then pulled out of his grip. "Well…" Still undecided, she wasn't sure what to tell him. "I, er." She looked down at the paper bag.

"I bought some material and patterns, but now I'm not so sure I have the skills or the time to make them." There, she'd said it.

He reached out for the package. "Let me see." He opened the bag, pulling out the contents. He studied the paper patterns, then checked the fabric. He flicked the fabrics open until they ran the full length of his cutting table, then studied them some more.

He looked Emily up and down again, and took some measurements, noting them in a book, not saying a word.

Joe indicated for her to sit while he did some calculations. Finally he lifted his head. "I'd love to do this for you, Emily. As a sign of our enduring friendship, I will give you a discounted rate."

She quickly stood. "Oh no! No, you mustn't." Her heart was racing. That wasn't what she wanted to achieve coming here to her friend for help.

He shushed her by putting a finger to her lips. "Here is an account for the three gowns." He handed her a sheet out of his account book. "It would normally be much more, but you've supplied the patterns and materials, so the price is far lower."

She hesitated. It didn't seem much for all the work involved. Each gown would take several days if she sewed them herself. Of course Joe had a sewing machine.

"The first one will be ready this time tomorrow if you decide to go ahead."

She liked the sound of that. "Yes, please do. It will save me such a lot of work."

He beamed. "I can already picture these beautiful fabrics on you. Next time, come here first – I have several fabrics the Mercantile cannot supply."

She nodded. What had she been thinking? Of course this was a far better option, and many of the local women came to Joe for their clothing needs. He called himself a tailor, but he did far more than men's suits.

"Perhaps," she said, glancing around the room at the beautiful fabrics he had. "You could make a some more gowns for me?"

His eyes lit up. "Of course, but the price will be higher since I'll be supplying the fabric."

She agreed, and they chose two different fabrics. Emily agreed to leave the designs up to Joe. She trusted him implicitly.

"Right. Come back around this time tomorrow, or later if it suits you better, and one gown will be done. Otherwise, give me at least a week to do them all."

Emily thought for a moment, her hand resting on her chin. "I'll see you tomorrow afternoon then." They said their goodbyes and she left the store, a song in her heart at the thought of a new wardrobe of clothes.

But more than that, the thought of what a new wardrobe would do to her spirits.

It had been far too long since she'd indulged herself like this. Her heart skipped a beat as Emily headed back to the boarding house.

* * *

True to his word, Joe had a package waiting for her when Emily returned the next day.

It contained not one, but two gowns – one was a simple house-gown, using one of the patterns she supplied, and the other was a little more fancy, and would be good for both church and special times with Patrick.

He insisted she try them both on to ensure they fitted correctly, which they did. Emily vividly remembered Joe from their school days. He was always meticulous with everything he did.

They'd been great friends, and she had been in awe of how smart he had been, particularly with mathematics. She was certain that would help with his work as a tailor.

Emily stared at herself in his full-length mirror, then twirled about. Tears came to her eyes at the vision she saw there.

"They're beautiful, Joe," she said, then reached out and hugged him.

He stepped back and stared into her face. "You deserve it, Emily. You've had a hard life, but I've heard on the grapevine Patrick Harper is changing all that."

She stared at him. "People are talking about me?" She was appalled. Gossip did not sit well with Emily.

He shook his head. "Not like that – word gets around. Everyone says he's a good man, and I hope they are right." He tugged at the gown ensuring it fit correctly in all the right places.

She smiled at the thought. "He is a good man. He's helped me tremendously in more ways than you will ever know."

Joe frowned. "Then why aren't you two married?"

Now it was her turn to frown. "He hasn't asked me." She glanced at herself in the mirror.

Joe shook his head at her words, then glanced at her reflection. "You look beautiful, Emily. This fabric brings out your beauty."

She grinned at him. "Now all I need is for Patrick to tell me so."

He was about to leave the room for her to change, when he turned back. "Why don't you leave that one on? Let your man see how beautiful you really are?"

Before she could answer he was gone. But he was right – why not leave it on and surprise Patrick when he arrived home from work?

As she left the store, Emily planted a quick kiss on Joe's cheek. "Thank you," she said quietly. "You are a good friend."

He reached out and took both her hands, staring her up and down. "And you, Emily Stanton, are a beautiful woman and a great catch." He grinned. "I just wish I had snatched you up when I had the chance."

She headed back home with a skip in her step.

* * *

Patrick headed straight for the bathroom when he arrived home.

He was becoming Sawdust Patrick, the way things were going. He'd cut so much wood this week, he felt like he had sawdust packed into every crevice.

He removed his shirt then covered his entire head in water and washed away the grime. He repeated the process for good measure.

This was the time of day he enjoyed the most – when he got to spend quality time with Emily.

When he'd changed into clean clothes, he headed for the kitchen to see the love of his life. He'd seen her at breakfast, but only briefly, before he'd had to leave for work.

As he stepped into the kitchen he abruptly stopped. He couldn't help but stare. He knew Emily was beautiful, but tonight she looked radiant.

What had she done differently?

"Hello, Patrick. Did you have a good day?" She grinned at him.

Did that mean she was happy to see him? "I missed you today." The moment the words were out of his mouth, he knew it wasn't enough. He rushed to her side and pulled her into his embrace. "You look beautiful tonight, Emily."

He hugged her a little tighter, then pulled back to kiss her. Emily's eyes sparkled. It was a moment to rejoice – finally she was on the road to recovery.

After a sweet lingering kiss, she pushed away. "I must finish preparing supper," she said, a note of regret in her voice.

He nodded. "I need to talk to you after supper, if you have time," he said.

She frowned. "Is everything alright?"

He reached out and took both her hands in his. "Everything is more than alright. Perhaps we can go for a stroll later?"

"I would love to."

He pulled the plates out of the cupboard ready for supper, as well as the mugs, then spread them across the counter. He always enjoyed being in Emily's kitchen. Apart from the enticing aromas, it was the woman herself. He had felt drawn to her from the moment they'd met.

"I'm about to dish up, if you'd care to tell the others?"

He wanted supper over and done with so he could talk to Emily in private. He didn't want the others around. What he had to say was none of their business.

He returned to find potato pancakes on each plate, with a side of bacon and sausages. He hadn't had that for a very long time and was looking forward to it, but not as much as their alone time.

The men each took a plate and a mug of coffee and headed for the dining room. The changes he'd implemented had made a huge difference to Emily, but were insignificant to her lodgers.

When only the two of them remained, Emily sidled up to him. "What did you want to talk about?" she asked quietly.

He reached out and cupped her face with his hands. "Nothing to worry your pretty little head about." He leaned in and brushed his lips against hers.

It left him reeling. That a gentle touch such as this could leave him feeling this way, sent shock waves through his entire body.

"You get the mugs, I'll carry the plates."

She nodded and headed out to the dining room where the lodgers were waiting to say grace. They seemed to have tamed quite a bit since Patrick arrived, and he wasn't unhappy about it.

There had been no new lodgers, as none had left. The changes made had ensured a happier house, which mean they didn't want to leave.

He sat down opposite Emily and they all bowed their heads.

They took turns saying grace, and tonight it was Patrick's turn.

"Dear Lord," Patrick began. "Thank you for this delicious food before us, and the amazing lady who prepared it. Amen."

Amen was echoed around the table. Emily blushed.

They all tucked in. The food was delicious as always, but Patrick couldn't wait for the meal to be over. He wanted to get on with it, but not with everyone here.

When she finished eating, Emily stood and carried her plate to the kitchen. Patrick followed.

He watched as she cut up a peach pie and distributed it over the bowls already laid out on the bench. She scooped up a big helping of clotted cream for each bowl.

Soon after the rest of the lodgers arrived in the kitchen, adding their dishes and cutlery to the sink, and snatching up a bowl and spoon.

"The food was delicious, Emily."

"Loved the pancakes."

"Nice meal."

She blushed at each compliment, and Patrick was pleased the lodgers now appreciated her the way she deserved.

He carried Emily's dessert for her.

"Emily and I are going for a stroll after supper," he announced when everyone was seated.

George looked around the table. "Don't worry about the dishes," he said. "We'll do them."

Emily frowned. "You don't have to do that."

"We don't mind," George said. "You enjoy your stroll with Patrick. We appreciate you more than you'll ever know."

Zachary Collard, who rarely said a word, spoke up. "I don't mind helping."

Patrick felt the warmth creep though his body. Finally, the message was getting through. They were all on a better than good thing, and didn't want to lose it.

The moment supper was over, Emily removed her apron and hung it on the hook in the kitchen. She rushed up stairs to freshen up, and to get a light shawl. The nights were becoming a little cooler.

Patrick waited for her at the bottom of the stairs. When she came into view, his heart thudded. She was so beautiful, both inside and out.

She hooked her arm in his and they headed out. "Where are we going?" she asked as he closed the door behind them.

"I thought we'd just stroll. Or perhaps a coffee at the diner?"

She stared at him. "We've just had supper."

"A stroll it is." He headed for the cottage he'd been working on recently. Emily hadn't seen it and he thought it might be of interest.

Since they were working along the same street, and would continue to do so for some time, Harry and Patrick had constructed a wooden bench to sit on during their breaks.

He headed straight there.

"Here we are," he said as they sat on the wooden bench.

"Where is *here*? I have no idea what this place is."

"This is where I've been working all these weeks. Harry and I have built all these cottages."

She stared at him. "Oooh, you are so clever! And they're so beautiful."

"Would you like to see inside?" He hoped she would say yes. There was one cottage in particular he wanted her to see.

"Is that alright? We won't get into trouble?"

He stood and pulled her up with him. "We won't get into trouble, I promise."

He held her hand and pulled her toward that one special cottage. "This one is still being built, but will have three bedrooms. One for the parents, and another two for any children who might happen along."

Emily looked confused.

He opened the front door and led her into a wide open space that would eventually become a sitting room. Right now it was just a shell.

She twirled around looking about. "It's beautiful. Whoever gets this cottage will be very lucky."

He suddenly dropped onto one knee, and Emily stared down at him, studying his face, and looking totally confused.

"What are you doing, Patrick? You need to get up."

She looked panicked, but he wasn't going to let that stop him in his quest. "Emily Stanton," he said, reaching for her left hand. "Will you marry me?"

He pulled out a small ring box from his pocket and opened it. He slid the ring on her finger before she had a chance to answer.

Emily stared down at the ring on her finger, her eyes filling with tears.

Panic began to fill him. She hadn't answered his question. "Emily?"

Her bottom lip quivered. This was not going to plan. His heart thudded in his chest. She was going to refuse him, he could feel it in his whole being.

He closed his eyes against the disappointment.

"Of course I'll marry you, Patrick, you goose. I love you."

He jumped to his feet and pulled her close, kissing her gently at first, then more urgently. It felt as though his entire body quivered at the revelation she would soon be his wife.

Finally, he pulled back.

"What do you think of the cottage," he asked, leading her through each room.

She stared in amazement. "It's beautiful. Whoever this belongs to is very lucky."

"I have a confession to make," he said as pulled away from her. "This cottage is ours. With Harry's help, I've been building it bit by bit. Saying behind later every night to get it done."

Tears streamed down her face. "I am very blessed," she said, before she buried her face into his shoulder.

* * *

Joe had finished all Emily's new gowns and she chose the fanciest of them all to be married in.

It was one of the gowns Joe had designed specifically for Emily, and she adored it. It was almost as though he knew she would be married in this particular gown.

It was to be a simple ceremony, but it seemed practically the entire town was there on this sunny Saturday afternoon. The wedding was less than a week since Patrick asked her to marry him, but neither of them wanted to wait.

As she walked down the aisle, Mrs Baker as her escort, she glanced about. All her lodgers were there, Daniel Carson from the Saw Mill, Joe, Cecil Delbert from the Mercantile, and many others.

Preacher Devon stood at the front of the church waiting for her to arrive. Patrick turned to face her, beaming with pride.

He wore his Sunday best suit.

His hands reached out to her as she reached the front, and Mrs Baker took a seat on the front pew.

The ceremony seemed to come and go in a blur, but Emily clearly remembered saying her vows and the preacher pronouncing them man and wife.

Patrick had arranged for Mrs Baker put on a small celebration for them after the ceremony. It wasn't huge, but finished off the day nicely.

The thing that had bothered Emily, about the future of the boarding house, had been resolved. They would stay there until their cottage was finished, and then they would hire a manager to run the place.

Emily was the happiest she had been for a long time.

Epilogue

Ten Months Later…

Patrick had worked hard to have their cottage completely finished in time for the baby's arrival.

Working on it only an hour or so a day, he'd only made it by a few weeks.

Doc Spencer had been inside with Emily for some hours, along with his wife, and Mrs Baker who was keeping him informed.

He sat on the wooden seat he and Harry had made what seemed forever ago, and worried about his wife's state of health.

He buried his head in his hands worrying, and looked up when he heard Mrs Baker walking toward him.

"You have a baby son," she said, tears in her eyes. "Come and meet your son. Emily will be happy to see you, too."

His heart pounded. He had a son. *He had a son!*

As he stepped into the bedroom, Emily smiled wearily up at him. He sat on the side of the bed and leaned in to kiss her. Their son was cradled in her arms and was greedily feeding from his mother.

"Meet your son," she said, tears filling her eyes. "What shall we call him? We didn't really choose any names."

He didn't have a clue. "Perhaps we could name him after your grandfather? After all, if it wasn't for him and his boarding house, we would never have met."

She looked thoughtful. "Winston Jonas Harper. It has a nice ring to it." Emily closed her eyes and nodded off to sleep as the baby continued to suckle.

Patrick pondered he was the luckiest man in the world, but realized they still had at least one more bedroom to fill.

He was not unhappy about the thought he might have to extent, or better yet, build a bigger cottage for his beautiful family.

He bowed his head and silently said a prayer of thanks to God for bringing him to Grand Falls, and especially for guiding him to his beautiful Emily.

From the Author

Thank you for reading *Emily*! I hope you enjoyed Emily and Patrick's story as much as I enjoyed writing it. The *Brides of Montana* series continues with *Grace*.

Books in this series are as follows:

Emily

Grace

Victoria

Maggie

Callie

Olivia

To find out about new books, sign up for my newsletter at:

cheryl-wright.com/newsletter/

About the Author

Multi-published, award-winning and bestselling author Cheryl Wright, former secretary, debt collector, account manager, writing coach, and shopping tour hostess, loves reading.

She writes both historical and contemporary western romance, as well as romantic suspense.

She lives in Melbourne, Australia, and is married with two adult children and has six grandchildren. When she's not writing, she can be found in her craft room making greeting cards.

Links

Website: *http://www.cheryl-wright.com/*

Facebook Reader Group:
https://www.facebook.com/groups/cherylwrightauthor/

Join My Newsletter:

https://cheryl-wright.com/newsletter/